HOW TO CATCH A GHOST

Written by Stuart A. Kallen

Published by Abdo & Daughters, 6535 Cecilia Circle, Edina, Minnesota
55439.

Library bound edition distributed by Rockbottom Books, Pentagon Tower,
P.O. Box 36036, Minneapolis, Minnesota 55435.

Library of Congress Number: 91-073063   ISBN: 1-56239-038-4
Cover Illustrated by: Tim Blough
Inside Illustrations by: Tim Blough

133.1

Edited by: Rosemary Wallner

TABLE OF CONTENTS

Part One

Part Two

PART ONE
THEY WALK AMONG US!

Somewhere betwixt this dimension and the next lies a world that is visited by spirits. Between the present and the past exists a well-traveled trail that shows us the way to our future. The past-living are what all of us shall become when we cease to breathe life into our lungs.

Ghosts haunt the four corners of the earth. From the highest mountaintop in Tibet to the deepest valleys of the Amazon. In the countries of Europe and the forests of America the spirits of the dead visit us daily. They are on a mission known only to themselves.

NO MATTER WHERE YOU LOOK

Sometimes ghosts make their presence known to us in harmless ways. A shadow in the dead of night. A cold spot in the hallway. Weird noises under the basement stairs.

The restless dead come to us in a variety of forms: a beautiful maiden hovering over the ocean; a ragged skeleton quaking in the closet; a headless soldier marching into a battle forever lost; or a long-dead king searching again for his kingdom.

All are undead souls in pursuit of a final peace.

ON A MISSION

The reasons that these spirits still inhabit our world are as varied as the ghosts themselves. Some ghosts come to complete unfinished business. Some ghosts come to correct wrongs that were done to them while they were alive. Some ghosts are forever doomed to restless wandering in a search for fleeting happiness. Some ghosts are called back to the earth by the living.

When ghosts visit humans, a few cause great harm as if seeking revenge. Floating through the woods at midnight, some evil phantoms terrorize and haunt any innocent person who crosses their path. But the truth is, most ghosts wander harmlessly through our human affairs, unaware and uncaring of their effects upon the living.

A LESSON TO BE LEARNED

Most people run in terror from ghosts. The sight of an ice-cold, pale-white cadaver knocking on a bedroom window would sap the courage from any brave soul. But the horrible image painted by some is an exaggerated story — more a product of misunderstanding than reality. The fact is that most ghosts are woefully ignorant of human beings.

Professional ghost hunters feel that there is much to be learned from studying phantasmagoria (fan-tas-ma-gor-eea). Instead of fearing ghosts, ghost hunters search out the awakened dead in hopes of bridging our two worlds.

Contained herein are a few hard, cold facts about ghosts, specters, apparitions, phantoms, and spooks.

DOWN THROUGH HISTORY

A skull in a shoe box causes all who move it outside to die within a year . . . A little bald man dressed in seventeenth century clothing leans over a bed and swings his arm. The person sleeping in the bed awakens with a black eye . . . A crew of World War I airmen appear with their airplane at a modern-day airport. They've all been dead for sixty years . . . A lawyer enters a meat market and throws slabs of meat across the floor. When the butchers try to stop him, their fists and knives pass right through him . . .

According to records, all of these ghostly events actually took place. What caused these things, no one knows. But the people who were there know what they saw, and they are not alone . . .

HISTORICALLY SPOOKING

Ghosts have made their mark on human affairs since the beginning of time. Their appearances have been recorded in the clay tablets of the Babylonians and the early writings of the Romans.

A crew of World War I airmen appear with their airplane at a modern day airport.

From the glyphs of the ancient Egyptians to the paintings of the Middle Ages, ghostly events have been recorded. They have been documented on antique cameras of the nineteenth century and on the high-tech cameras of today. Images of ghosts have been drawn, carved, painted, and photographed by faithful believers whose lives have been touched.

According to the dictionary, a ghost is defined as "a disembodied spirit of a dead person wandering among or haunting living persons." The word "ghost" came from the Old English word "guest." And England is full of stories of haunted "guests" visiting the living!

The reports of ghost sightings throughout history would fill hundreds of volumes, and yet no one has ever proved that ghosts really exist. As professional ghost hunter Dr. Samual Johnson states, "All argument is against it, but all belief is for it."

A VARIETY OF PHANTOMS

Although people can't agree on what a ghost is, skilled ghost hunters do agree that ghosts appear for several reasons, and come in many forms. Here are some varieties of spooks from a ghost hunter's notebook:

LIGHT PARTICLE GHOSTS

When an especially tragic or violent event takes place, the image of the event is left in the air by electrical charges released from the dying person. The weather might have something to do with this strange phenomenon. Such events remain as light particles, vibrating for many years, possibly forever.

These electrical impressions are usually seen by people after a sudden drop in temperature. Spooky noises such as footsteps, screaming, and the swish of clothing may be heard. Sometimes the ghosts replay an actual event, such as a hanging or a phantom army marching. These types of ghosts eventually fade, sometimes leaving behind their sounds after their image's have disappeared.

HISTORICAL GHOSTS

Ghosts that appear to walk through walls, dress in antique clothing, and ignore their living counterparts are known as historical ghosts. These ghosts are sighted in very old houses and castles. Gliding through hallways and passages that were familiar to them when they were alive, historical apparitions are the most commonly sighted ghosts.

When houses have had rooms added, floors raised, and ceilings lowered, the ghosts will appear to glide through the walls. They may only appear from the knees up or the neck down. This is because they are walking through passages long since changed. Historical phantoms never speak and rarely sense the presence of human beings. Usually historical ghosts have suffered some great tragedy in their lifetimes. Often, these ghosts come to be treated as "one of the family" by the people who live in the ancient structures that the phantoms haunt.

Historical ghosts appear to walk through walls, wear antique clothing and ignore their human counterparts.

13

MODERN GHOSTS

The ghost of Bob Loft, the pilot on Eastern Airlines Flight 401 has been seen on more than twenty occasions. Flight 401 crashed into a Florida swamp in 1972 killing all 101 people aboard. Loft and his copilot, Don Repo, have been seen as lifelike figures by flight attendants and crew members. Some of these people knew the pilots, some identified them in pictures.

Ghosts can be seen by anybody at any time of the day or night. Sometimes the ghosts have been dead for centuries, sometimes for only a few hours and sometimes NOT DEAD AT ALL!

GHOSTS OF THE LIVING

At the opening battle of the English Civil War in 1642, Prince Rupert led his cavalry into battle. For years afterward, people claimed to see a ghostly replay of the battle. Everyone who saw it agreed that Prince Rupert was the ghost who was leading the charge . . . but he was still alive! There are thousands of such recorded incidents.

You pass a friend on a street only to find out later that they were miles away. A person wakes suddenly in the night and sees a familiar shadow standing by the window; it is the shadow of a relative who lives across the ocean.

These sightings may have to do with "astral travel." This may occur when a person wishes to visit a trusting friend who lives far away. Although they are separated by miles, their "astral souls" have left their physical bodies and are having an encounter in another dimension.

GHOSTS OF THE DYING

During both World Wars, it was common for wives and mothers to "see" their husbands and sons who were soldiers in an army thousands of miles away. Later, these women would find out that their loved ones had been killed in battle at the time of the sighting.

Apparitions of the dying usually last for only several hours. It is reasoned that when a person is dying, they think strongly of their loved ones, and telepathically send an image of themselves to those people.

Lady Dorothy Walpole met a violent end on the staircase where her ghost has been photographed floating around.

16

ALL IN THE FAMILY GHOSTS

For some people, ghosts run in the family. In England and Scotland, it is not uncommon for a long line of Pomeroys or Walpoles to have one or more ghosts haunting their castles for centuries. King George IV and others have sighted the Famous Brown Lady in Pomeroy Castle. Although no one knows her exact ancestry, some people think she is Lady Dorothy Walpole. Lady Walpole is said to have met a violent end on the staircase where she has been seen and photographed.

WOMEN OF FAIRY FOLK

The term "howling like a Banshee" comes from the British Isles. When a person in an ancient Irish family was close to death, an eerie howling and shrieking was heard around his or her deathbed. Swirling through the walls and floors came a terrifying howl that proceded death. The female ghosts singing these mournful tunes were known as "Banshees." They were thought to be family members who had died in earlier times.

GHOSTLY OBJECTS

A foolish hitchhiker sat down in the Haunted Stoop ("stoop" is an English word for chair) at Busby Stoop Inn in Yorkshire, England. Within two days he was dead. At least a dozen other people have died within a week of sitting in the chair belonging to Busby.

Busby was a thief and a murderer who lived in the nineteenth century. When he was finally sentenced to death, the police entered his home to bring him to justice. Busby was dragged kicking and screaming from his favorite chair.

"Any person who sits in my favorite stoop will die as quickly and violently as I am about to die!" shrieked Busby as he was led away.

Busby's words have rung true. Many people have died suddenly after sitting in Busby's stoop. The haunted chair was finally removed from Busby Stoop Inn.

Busby's chair is one among thousands of known "haunted objects." Human skulls are thought to have great power; they work their magic anywhere that they are stored. In England there is a skull of a prehistoric girl in a shoe box in Bettiscombe Manor. It is said to scream and cause farmers' crops to fail if it is taken outside.

18

Busby was dragged kicking and screaming from his favorite chair. At least a dozen people have died who have sat in Busby's stoop.

Death will come within a year, to the person who commits that deed.

Ghost ships have been seen floating on winds by sailors on all the Seven Seas.

WRAPPING IT UP

No one knows if this list of ghost types is complete. Some ghosts overlap in several catagories. Some ghosts are people experiencing life after death. There are ghosts of animals ranging from dogs and cats, to horses, sheep, and even bears! When the curtain between this world and the ghost world is parted, anything is possible.

PART TWO
CATCH A GHOST!
FINDING A PHANTOM

If you want to find yourself a ghost, you need to go where the ghosts gather. Most spooks are spotted where death or an act of violence has occurred. A little research at your library may turn up articles and books about haunted hangouts in your town. Some libraries keep a "ghost file" that contains information about local ghosts. Ask your librarian.

If you want to seek out spooks on your own, the following list of places should help you:

* *Old Houses* — If you or one of your friends live in an old house, you are in luck. Over the years, many people have lived and died there. Most houses are not haunted, however, so finding an old house doesn't mean you will find a ghost, but it is a good place to start. New houses may be haunted if they were built on the sight of a hanging or battle, or if a ghost has haunted that area before.

* *Battlefields* — Many places in the world have been the sight of violent battles. The battlefield at Shiloh, Tennessee, is said to be haunted. In the Civil War, during two days of fighting in April 1862, over 24,000 men died in the bloody battle of Shiloh. In the years that followed, people witnessed a phantom battle where they heard gunshots, sabres clashing, and the screams and shouts of the dying men. Shiloh is said to be haunted to this very day.

  If you do not live near Civil War battlefields, you might live near the sight of Native American, Revolutionary War, or War of 1812 battles. In Europe, there are many battlefields from the Middle Ages to World Wars I and II. Once again, a trip to your library should give you the information you need to find a nearby battlefield.

* *Graveyards* — A cemetery seems like a natural place to find ghosts until you realize that most ghosts haunt the places where they died. Very few people die in graveyards — unless it's from fright! Some graveyards are thought to have "graveyard guardians." This is the spirit of the first person buried there. The guardian's task is

to keep away evil spirits and unwanted intruders. In ancient times, sometimes a living person was sacrificed when a new burial ground was established. This insured that the graveyard would have its guardian. Those were the ghoul old days!

* *Historical Public Buildings* — Almost every town has public buildings that were once privately owned homes. Europe has hundreds of castles that are now open to the public. Many of these castles have torture chambers and hanging grounds that are known to be haunted. In the United States, many towns have museums, government buildings, abandoned prisons, and even schools where frightening phantoms have been found.

The New York state capitol in Albany is said to be haunted by Samuel Abbott, a night watchman who died there in 1911. After a fire burned down the west wing of the capitol building, all that was found of Abbott were his boots and belt buckle. For seventy years, janitors, security guards, and maintenance workers heard jangling keys, heavy breathing, furniture moving, and doorknobs turning. They said the noises were made by "old Abbott."

Abbott's ghost was finally exorcized (expelled) by a professional ghost hunter at a seance in 1981. After two loud bangs sounded and a cold gust of wind blew through the room, Abbott's agony was finally put to an end.

People conduct seance's to talk with or contact spirits.

* *Roads and Highways* — Sharp curves, steep cliffs, and dangerous intersections are the sights of many car crashes. Some places have had dozens of collisions over a long period of time. Many a driver has seen a creepy corpse restlessly roaming the sight of a smashup from long ago. Was it the driver's tired eyes playing tricks? Or was it the undead, warning the living to be careful lest they suffer the same fate?

HOW TO SPOT A SPOOK

Being a ghost hunter might be one of the toughest jobs in the world. Most of the time ghost hunters sit in the dark all night, fighting off sleep. Usually they never even see a spook. On the rare occasions when a spook does appear, excitement and research of the undead is the reward for the ghost hunter's patience.

Some ghost hunters drag five-hundred-pound trunks full of high-tech gizmos to the haunted sight. Others make do with just a few handy items. Whichever way you approach ghost hunting, just remember, only a ghost can decide when and where it will wander. Just hope you have the ghostly luck to be there when it happens.

TOOLS OF THE TRADE

Now that you know all about ghosts and where to hunt for them, you will need some basic equipment for your task. Most of these items can be found around the house. After you assemble your ghost hunter's tools, a-hunting we will ghost.

Start with a bag or old suitcase to hold everything, then find:

* A pad of paper and a pencil

* A tape measure

* A roll of black thread

* A roll of masking tape

* Rubber cement

* Thumbtacks

* A small sack of flour

* A flashlight

* A tape recorder (optional)

* A camera and tripod (optional)

* A book

THE HUNT IS ON

The best place to practice ghost hunting is at your home or the home of a relative or friend. If you know someone who thinks they have seen a ghost, check out their sighting. Most people see ghosts in or near their own home. The attic, basement, or garage is a good place to start. Any out-of-the-way room or even your bedroom may be haunted.

CONDUCT AN INTERVIEW

Unpack your ghost kit, and start with your pencil and paper. If you know someone who has seen a ghost, interview him or her. If you have a tape recorder, record the interview. Ask the ghost sighter the exact details of the sighting. Find out the time of day that the ghost was seen and the ghost's age. Find out what kind of clothing the ghost was wearing and the type of movement.

Was the ghost looking out the window? Gliding through the air? Dancing? Wandering aimlessly? Was there any communcation between the ghost and the viewer? Was the ghost happy or sad?

Crying? Angry? Troubled? Finally, where and when did the ghost disappear? Did it walk through the wall? Fly through the ceiling?

After you have recorded these answers, interview other people who live in the area and ask them if they have ever seen the ghost. Each person should be interviewed alone so that their answers are not changed by the presence of others.

Once you have conducted your interviews, go to the sight of the haunting. Use your tape measure to draw a map of the room to scale. Make one foot equal to one square on the paper. Draw the path the ghost took through the room and where it disappeared.

SECURE THE ROOM

Next, examine the room carefully. If the ghost seemed to disappear through a wall, check the area for loose floorboards. Has the wall been altered or rebuilt? Has the ceiling been lowered? Remember, many times ghosts wander through walls that were not there at the time of their deaths.

Using a tape measure to draw a map of the room to scale.

You must now make the room secure so that only a ghost could enter and leave it. This is where you will need your tape and thread. First, place small dabs of rubber cement on the door frame about six inches off the ground. (Rubber cement will rub off after you are finished and will not damage the paint.) Stretch the thread across the doorway and stick it to the rubber cement. If this is difficult, push thumbtacks in the door frame and wrap the thread around them. If a human walks in the room, they will break the thread. If a ghost enters, the thread will remain in place.

Now run the masking tape across all the windows so that if the window is opened, the tape will be broken. Make sure all doors and windows are sealed with thread and tape. If the ghost has been moving furniture, tape small pieces of paper to the floor under the legs of chairs and tables. Draw a circle on the paper around the legs of the furniture. If anything moves, you will be able to see it.

Finally, sprinkle flour on the floor by the doors, windows, and the path that the ghost was said to have walked. Ghosts leave no footprints, so the flour should remain undisturbed.

GHOSTLY STAKEOUT

Now you are ready to settle in for the night. Reading a book with your flashlight is a good way to relax and take your mind off of your surroundings. Many people have seen ghosts when they looked up after being "lost" in a book. Another way to relax is to lie down. Over twenty-five percent of people who have seen ghosts reported the sighting a few hours after they had fallen asleep and were suddenly awakened. Of course, you don't want to sleep through the sighting, so use your judgement here.

If you don't see a ghost right away just remember that most people don't spot ghosts on their first try. If you hang out at the right haunts and keep trying to find phantoms, sooner or later you will succeed. Until then, happy haunting and ghoul luck!